Buster blinked his greedy little eyes rapidly and looked again. Frontispiece. *See page 65.*

CHILDREN'S THRIFT CLASSICS

The Adventures of Buster Bear

THORNTON W. BURGESS

Original Illustrations by Harrison Cady
Adapted by Thea Kliros

PUBLISHED IN ASSOCIATION WITH THE
THORNTON W. BURGESS MUSEUM AND THE
GREEN BRIAR NATURE CENTER, SANDWICH, MASSACHUSETTS,
BY
DOVER PUBLICATIONS, INC., NEW YORK

DOVER CHILDREN'S THRIFT CLASSICS
Editor: Philip Smith

Published in Canada by General Publishing Company, Ltd., 30 Lesmill Road, Don Mills, Toronto, Ontario.
Published in the United Kingdom by Constable and Company, Ltd., 3 The Lanchesters, 162–164 Fulham Palace Road, London W6 9ER.

This Dover edition, first published in 1993 in association with the Thornton W. Burgess Museum and the Green Briar Nature Center, Sandwich, Massachusetts, who have provided a new introduction, is an unabridged republication of the work first published by Little, Brown, and Company, Boston, in 1916. The original halftone illustrations by Harrison Cady have been adapted in line format by Thea Kliros for this edition.

Manufactured in the United States of America
Dover Publications, Inc., 31 East 2nd Street, Mineola, N.Y. 11501

Library of Congress Cataloging-in-Publication Data

Burgess, Thornton W. (Thornton Waldo), 1874–1965.
    The adventures of Buster Bear / Thornton W. Burgess ; original illustrations by Harrison Cady ; adapted by Thea Kliros.
        p.   cm. — (Dover children's thrift classics)
    Summary: The other animals are frightened when Buster Bear comes to live in the Green Forest, until he gets into trouble trying to steal blueberries from Farmer Brown's boy and they realize he is not very different from them.
    ISBN 0-486-27564-7
    [1. Bears—Fiction. 2. Animals—Fiction.] I. Cady, Harrison, 1877–   , ill. II. Kliros, Thea, ill. III. Title. IV. Series.
PZ7.B917Aah   1993
[Fic]—dc20   92–36949
                                                    CIP
                                                    AC

Introduction to the Dover Edition

WITH HIS huge footprints and his "grumbly-rumbly" voice, Buster Bear struck fear in the hearts of all the creatures who lived in the Green Forest upon his arrival there. But when they saw Buster get into trouble trying to steal blueberries from Farmer Brown's boy, they realized that their new neighbor was not so very different from the rest of them. Even Little Joe Otter discovered that Buster had a jovial sense of humor.

The Adventures of Buster Bear, first published in 1916, was the work of author, naturalist and environmentalist Thornton W. Burgess. Born in Sandwich, Massachusetts, in 1874, he wandered the shores, meadows and forests of this Cape Cod town during his boyhood, gaining a love and appreciation of nature that formed the spirit of his later work. From his first book in 1910 to this day, the stories of Thornton Burgess have delighted both young and old. But Burgess did more than just entertain: he was careful to present accurately the habits of wild creatures so that readers would also learn from his stories. He further believed that children could gain a better understanding of life by reading about the ways of the animals. It was his aim that those who read his stories would grow to share his love of nature and his concern for the natural environment and its preservation.

Today that aim is the stated goal of the Thornton W. Burgess Society in Sandwich. The Society runs the Thornton W. Burgess Museum, which honors the life and work of this extraordinary man, and the Green Briar Nature Center, which carries out his goals in environmental education and preservation.

Contents

List of Illustrations

I

Buster Bear Goes Fishing

BUSTER BEAR yawned as he lay on his comfortable bed of leaves and watched the first early morning sunbeams creeping through the Green Forest to chase out the Black Shadows. Once more he yawned, and slowly got to his feet and shook himself. Then he walked over to a big pine-tree, stood up on his hind legs, reached as high up on the trunk of the tree as he could, and scratched the bark with his great claws. After that he yawned until it seemed as if his jaws would crack, and then sat down to think what he wanted for breakfast.

While he sat there, trying to make up his mind what would taste best, he was listening to the sounds that told of the waking of all the little people who live in the Green Forest. He heard Sammy Jay way off in the distance screaming, "Thief! Thief!" and grinned. "I wonder," thought Buster, "if some one has stolen Sammy's breakfast, or if he has stolen the breakfast of some one else. Probably he is the thief himself."

He heard Chatterer the Red Squirrel scolding as fast as he could make his tongue go and working himself into a terrible rage. "Must be that Chatterer got out of bed the wrong way this morning," thought he.

He heard Blacky the Crow cawing at the top of his lungs, and he knew by the sound that Blacky was getting into mischief of some kind. He heard the sweet voices of happy little singers, and they were good to hear. But most of all he listened to a merry, low, silvery laugh that never stopped but went on and on, until he just felt as if he must laugh too. It was the voice of the Laughing Brook. And as Buster listened it suddenly came to him just what he wanted for breakfast.

"I'm going fishing," said he in his deep grumbly-rumbly voice to no one in particular. "Yes, Sir, I'm going fishing. I want some fat trout for my breakfast."

He shuffled along over to the Laughing Brook, and straight to a little pool of which he knew, and as he drew near he took the greatest care not to make the teeniest, weeniest bit of noise. Now it just happened that early as he was, some one was before Buster Bear. When he came in sight of the little pool, who should he see but another fisherman there, who had already caught a fine fat trout. Who was it? Why, Little Joe Otter to be sure. He was just climbing up the bank with the fat trout in his mouth. Buster Bear's own mouth watered as he saw it. Little Joe sat down on the bank and prepared to enjoy his breakfast. He hadn't seen Buster Bear, and he didn't know that he or any one else was anywhere near.

Buster Bear tiptoed up very softly until he was right behind Little Joe Otter. "Woof, woof!" said he in his deepest, most grumbly-rumbly voice. "That's a very fine looking trout. I wouldn't mind if I had it myself."

Little Joe Otter gave a frightened squeal and without even turning to see who was speaking dropped his fish and dived headfirst into the Laughing Brook. Buster Bear sprang forward and with one of his big paws caught the fat trout just as it was slipping back into the water.

"Here's your trout, Mr. Otter," said he, as Little Joe put his head out of water to see who had frightened him so. "Come and get it."

But Little Joe wouldn't. The fact is, he was afraid to. He snarled at Buster Bear and called him a thief and everything bad he could think of. Buster didn't seem to mind. He chuckled

"Here's your trout, Mr. Otter," said he.
Page 3.

as if he thought it all a great joke and repeated his invitation to Little Joe to come and get his fish. But Little Joe just turned his back and went off down the Laughing Brook in a great rage.

"It's too bad to waste such a fine fish," said Buster thoughtfully. "I wonder what I'd better do with it." And while he was wondering, he ate it all up. Then he started down the Laughing Brook to try to catch some for himself.

II

Little Joe Otter Gets Even with Buster Bear

LITTLE JOE OTTER was in a terrible rage. It was a bad beginning for a beautiful day and Little Joe knew it. But who wouldn't be in a rage if his breakfast was taken from him just as he was about to eat it? Anyway, that is what Little Joe told Billy Mink. Perhaps he didn't tell it quite exactly as it was, but you know he was very badly frightened at the time.

"I was sitting on the bank of the Laughing

Brook beside one of the little pools," he told Billy Mink, "and was just going to eat a fat trout I had caught, when who should come along but that great big bully, Buster Bear. He took that fat trout away from me and ate it just as if it belonged to him! I hate him! If I live long enough I'm going to get even with him!"

Of course that wasn't nice talk and anything but a nice spirit, but Little Joe Otter's temper is sometimes pretty short, especially when he is hungry, and this time he had had no break-fast, you know.

Buster Bear hadn't actually taken the fish away from Little Joe. But looking at the mat-ter as Little Joe did, it amounted to the same thing. You see, Buster knew perfectly well when he invited Little Joe to come back and get it that Little Joe wouldn't dare do anything of the kind.

"Where is he now?" asked Billy Mink.

"He's somewhere up the Laughing Brook. I wish he'd fall in and get drowned!" snapped Little Joe.

Billy Mink just had to laugh. The idea of great big Buster Bear getting drowned in the Laughing Brook was too funny. There wasn't water enough in it anywhere except down in the Smiling Pool, and that was on the Green

Meadows, where Buster had never been known to go. "Let's go see what he is doing," said Billy Mink.

At first Little Joe didn't want to, but at last his curiosity got the better of his fear, and he agreed. So the two little brown-coated scamps turned down the Laughing Brook, taking the greatest care to keep out of sight themselves. They had gone only a little way when Billy Mink whispered: "Sh-h! There he is."

Sure enough, there was Buster Bear sitting close beside a little pool and looking into it very intently.

"What's he doing?" asked Little Joe Otter, as Buster Bear sat for the longest time without moving.

Just then one of Buster's big paws went into the water as quick as a flash and scooped out a trout that had ventured too near.

"He's fishing!" exclaimed Billy Mink.

And that is just what Buster Bear was doing, and it was very plain to see that he was having great fun. When he had eaten the trout he had caught, he moved along to the next little pool.

"They are *our* fish!" said Little Joe fiercely. "He has no business catching *our* fish!"

"I don't see how we are going to stop him," said Billy Mink.

"I do!" cried Little Joe, into whose head an idea had just popped. "I'm going to drive all the fish out of the little pools and muddy the water all up. Then we'll see how many fish he will get! Just you watch me get even with Buster Bear."

Little Joe slipped swiftly into the water and swam straight to the little pool that Buster Bear would try next. He frightened the fish so that they fled in every direction. Then he stirred up the mud until the water was so dirty that Buster couldn't have seen a fish right under his nose. He did the same thing in the next pool and the next. Buster Bear's fishing was spoiled for that day.

III

Buster Bear Is
Greatly Puzzled

BUSTER BEAR hadn't enjoyed himself so much since he came to the Green Forest to live. His fun began when he surprised Little Joe Otter on the bank of a little pool in the Laughing Brook and Little Joe was so frightened that he dropped a fat trout he had just caught. It had seemed like a great joke to Buster Bear, and he had chuckled over it all the time he was eating the fat trout. When he had finished it, he started on to do some fishing himself.

Presently he came to another little pool. He stole up to it very, very softly, so as not to frighten the fish. Then he sat down close to the edge of it and didn't move. Buster learned a long time ago that a fisherman must be patient unless, like Little Joe Otter, he is just as much at home in the water as the fish themselves, and can swim fast enough to catch them by chasing them. So he didn't move so much as an eye lash. He was so still that he looked almost like the stump of an old tree. Perhaps that is what the fish thought he was, for pretty soon, two or three swam right in close to where he was sitting. Now Buster Bear may be big and clumsy looking, but there isn't anything that can move much quicker than one of those big paws of his when he wants it to. One of them moved now, and quicker than a wink had scooped one of those foolish fish out on to the bank.

Buster's little eyes twinkled, and he smacked his lips as he moved on to the next little pool, for he knew that it was of no use to stay longer at the first one. The fish were so frightened that they wouldn't come back for a long, long time. At the next little pool the same thing happened. By this time Buster Bear was in fine spirits. It was fun to catch the fish, and it was still more fun to eat them. What finer breakfast could any one have than fresh-caught trout? No wonder he felt good! But it takes more than three trout to fill Buster Bear's stomach, so he kept on to the next little pool.

But this little pool, instead of being beautiful and clear so that Buster could see right to the bottom of it and so tell if there were any fish there, was so muddy that he couldn't see into it at all. It looked as if some one had just stirred up all the mud at the bottom.

"Huh!" said Buster Bear. "It's of no use to try to fish here. I would just waste my time. I'll try the next pool."

So he went on to the next little pool. He found this just as muddy as the other. Then he went on to another, and this was no better. Buster sat down and scratched his head. It was puzzling. Yes, Sir, it was puzzling. He looked this way and he looked that way suspiciously, but there was no one to be seen. Everything was still save for the laughter of the Laughing Brook. Somehow, it seemed to Buster as if the Brook were laughing at him.

"It's very curious," muttered Buster, "very curious indeed. It looks as if my fishing is spoiled for to-day. I don't understand it at all. It's lucky I caught what I did. It looks as if somebody is trying to—ha!" A sudden thought had popped into his head. Then he began to chuckle and finally to laugh. "I do believe that scamp Joe Otter is trying to get even with me for eating that fat trout!"

And then, because Buster Bear always enjoys a good joke even when it is on himself, he laughed until he had to hold his sides, which is a whole lot better than going off in a rage as Little Joe Otter had done. "You're pretty smart, Mr. Otter! You're pretty smart, but there are other people who are smart too," said Buster Bear, and still chuckling, he went off to think up a plan to get the best of Little Joe Otter.

IV

Little Joe Otter Supplies Buster Bear with a Breakfast

Getting even just for spite
Doesn't always pay.
Fact is, it is very apt
To work the other way.

THAT IS just how it came about that Little Joe Otter furnished Buster Bear with the best breakfast he had had for a long time. He didn't mean to do it. Oh, my, no! The truth is, he thought all the time that he was preventing Buster Bear from getting a breakfast. You see he wasn't well enough acquainted with Buster to know that Buster is quite as smart as he is, and perhaps a little bit smarter. Spite and selfishness were at the bottom of it. You see Little Joe and Billy Mink had had all the fishing in the Laughing Brook to themselves so long that they thought no one else had any right to fish there. To be sure Bobby Coon caught a few little fish there, but they didn't mind Bobby. Farmer Brown's boy fished there too, sometimes, and this always made Little Joe and Billy Mink very angry, but they were so afraid of him that they didn't dare do anything about it. But when they discovered that Buster Bear was a fisherman, they made up their minds that something had got to be done. At least, Little Joe did.

"He'll try it again to-morrow morning," said Little Joe. "I'll keep watch, and as soon as I see him coming, I'll drive out all the fish, just as I did to-day. I guess that'll teach him to let our fish alone."

So the next morning Little Joe hid before daylight close by the little pool where Buster Bear had given him such a fright. Sure enough, just as the Jolly Sunbeams began to creep through the Green Forest, he saw Buster Bear coming straight over to the little pool. Little Joe slipped into the water and chased all the fish out of the little pool, and stirred up the mud on the bottom so that the water was so muddy that the bottom couldn't be seen at all. Then he hurried down to the next little pool and did the same thing.

Now Buster Bear is very smart. You know he had guessed the day before who had spoiled his fishing. So this morning he only went far enough to make sure that if Little Joe were watching for him, as he was sure he would be, he would see him coming. Then, instead of keeping on to the little pool, he hurried to a place way down the Laughing Brook, where the water was very shallow, hardly over his feet, and there he sat chuckling to himself. Things happened just as he had expected. The frightened fish Little Joe chased out of the little pools up above swam down the Laughing Brook, because, you know, Little Joe was behind them, and there was nowhere else for them to go. When they came to the place where Buster was waiting, all he had to do was to scoop them out on to the bank. It was great fun. It didn't take Buster long to catch all the fish he could eat. Then he saved a nice fat trout and waited.

By and by along came Little Joe Otter, chuckling to think how he had spoiled Buster Bear's fishing. He was so intent on looking behind him to see if Buster was coming that he didn't see Buster waiting there until he spoke.

"I'm much obliged for the fine breakfast you have given me," said Buster in his deepest, most grumbly-rumbly voice. "I've saved a fat trout for you to make up for the one I ate yesterday. I hope we'll go fishing together often."

Then he went off laughing fit to kill himself. Little Joe couldn't find a word to say. He was so surprised and angry that he went off by himself and sulked. And Billy Mink, who had been watching, ate the fat trout.

V

Grandfather Frog's
Common Sense

THERE IS NOTHING quite like common sense to smooth out troubles. People who have plenty of just plain common sense are often thought to be very wise. Their neighbors look up to them and are forever running to them for advice, and they are very much respected. That is the way with Grandfather Frog. He is very old and very wise. Anyway, that is what his neighbors think. The truth is, he simply has a lot of common sense, which after all is the very best kind of wisdom.

Now when Little Joe Otter found that Buster Bear had been too smart for him and that instead of spoiling Buster's fishing in the Laughing Brook he had really made it easier for Buster to catch all the fish he wanted, Little Joe went off down to the Smiling Pool in a great rage.

Billy Mink stopped long enough to eat the fat fish Buster had left on the bank and then he too went down to the Smiling Pool.

When Little Joe Otter and Billy Mink reached the Smiling Pool, they climbed up on the Big Rock, and there Little Joe sulked and sulked, until finally Grandfather Frog asked what the matter was. Little Joe wouldn't tell, but Billy Mink told the whole story. When he told how Buster had been too smart for Little Joe, it tickled him so that Billy had to laugh in spite of himself. So did Grandfather Frog. So did Jerry Muskrat, who had been listening. Of course this made Little Joe angrier than ever. He said a lot of unkind things about Buster Bear and about Billy Mink and Grandfather Frog and Jerry Muskrat, because they had laughed at the smartness of Buster.

"He's nothing but a great big bully and thief!" declared Little Joe.

"Chug-a-rum! He may be a bully, because great big people are very apt to be bullies, and though I haven't seen him, I guess Buster Bear is big enough from all I have heard, but I don't see how he is a thief," said Grandfather Frog.

"Didn't he catch my fish and eat them?" snapped Little Joe. "Doesn't that make him a thief?"

"They were no more your fish than mine," protested Billy Mink.

"Well, *our* fish, then! He stole *our* fish, if you like that any better. That makes him just as much a thief, doesn't it?" growled Little Joe.

"You take my advice, Little Joe Otter,"
continued Grandfather Frog. *Page 18.*

Grandfather Frog looked up at jolly, round, bright Mr. Sun and slowly winked one of his great, goggly eyes. "There comes a foolish green fly," said he. "Who does he belong to?"

"Nobody!" snapped Little Joe. "What have foolish green flies got to do with my—I mean *our* fish?"

"Nothing, nothing at all," replied Grandfather Frog mildly. "I was just hoping that he would come near enough for me to snap him up; then he would belong to me. As long as he doesn't, he doesn't belong to any one. I suppose that if Buster Bear should happen along and catch him, he would be stealing from me, according to Little Joe."

"Of course not! What a silly idea! You're getting foolish in your old age," retorted Little Joe.

"Can you tell me the difference between the fish that you haven't caught and the foolish green flies that I haven't caught?" asked Grandfather Frog.

Little Joe couldn't find a word to say.

"You take my advice, Little Joe Otter," continued Grandfather Frog, "and always make friends with those who are bigger and stronger and smarter than you are. You'll find it pays."

VI

Little Joe Otter Takes Grandfather Frog's Advice

Who makes an enemy a friend,
To fear and worry puts an end.

LITTLE JOE OTTER found that out when he took Grandfather Frog's advice. He wouldn't have admitted that he was afraid of Buster Bear. No one ever likes to admit being afraid, least of all Little Joe Otter. And really Little Joe has a great deal of courage. Very few of the little people of the Green Forest or the Green Meadows would willingly quarrel with him, for Little Joe is a great fighter when he has to fight. As for all those who live in or along the Laughing Brook or in the Smiling Pool, they let Little Joe have his own way in everything.

Now having one's own way too much is a bad thing. It is apt to make one selfish and thoughtless of other people and very hard to get along with. Little Joe Otter had his way too much. Grandfather Frog knew it and shook his head very soberly when Little Joe had been disrespectful to him.

"Too bad. Too bad! Too bad! Chug-a-rum! It is too bad that such a fine young fellow as Little Joe should spoil a good disposition by such selfish heedlessness. Too bad," said he.

So, though he didn't let on that it was so, Grandfather Frog really was delighted when he heard how Buster Bear had been too smart for Little Joe Otter. It tickled him so that he had hard work to keep a straight face. But he did and was as grave and solemn as you please as he advised Little Joe always to make friends with any one who was bigger and stronger and smarter than he. That was good common sense advice, but Little Joe just sniffed and went off declaring that he would get even with Buster Bear yet. Now Little Joe is good-natured and full of fun as a rule, and after he had reached home and his temper had cooled off a little, he began to see the joke on himself,—how when he had worked so hard to frighten the fish in the little pools of the Laughing Brook so that Buster Bear should not catch any, he had all the time been driving them right into Buster's paws. By and by he grinned. It was a little sheepish grin at first, but at last it grew into a laugh.

"I believe," said Little Joe as he wiped tears of laughter from his eyes, "that Grandfather Frog is right, and that the best thing I can do is to make friends with Buster Bear. I'll try it to-morrow morning."

So very early the next morning Little Joe Otter went to the best fishing pool he knew of in the Laughing Brook, and there he caught the biggest trout he could find. It was so big and fat that it made Little Joe's mouth water, for you know fat trout are his favorite food. But he didn't take so much as one bite. Instead he carefully laid it on an old log where Buster Bear would be sure to see it if he should come along that way. Then he hid near by, where he could watch. Buster was late that morning. It seemed to Little Joe that he never would come. Once he nearly lost the fish. He had turned his head for just a minute, and when he looked back again, the trout was nowhere to be seen. Buster couldn't have stolen up and taken it, because such a big fellow couldn't possibly have gotten out of sight again.

Little Joe darted over to the log and looked on the other side. There was the fat trout, and there also was Little Joe's smallest cousin, Shadow the Weasel, who is a great thief and altogether bad. Little Joe sprang at him angrily, but Shadow was too quick and darted away. Little Joe put the fish back on the log and waited. This time he didn't take his eyes off it. At last, when he was almost ready to give up, he saw Buster Bear shuffling along towards the Laughing Brook. Suddenly Buster stopped and sniffed. One of the Merry Little Breezes had carried the scent of that fat trout over to him. Then he came straight over to where the fish lay, his nose wrinkling, and his eyes twinkling with pleasure.

"Now I wonder who was so thoughtful as to leave this fine breakfast ready for me," said he out loud.

"Me," said Little Joe in a rather faint voice. "I caught it especially for you."

"Thank you," replied Buster, and his eyes twinkled more than ever. "I think we are going to be friends."

"I—I hope so," replied Little Joe.

VII

Farmer Brown's Boy Has
No Luck at All

FARMER BROWN'S BOY tramped through the Green Forest, whistling merrily. He always whistles when he feels light-hearted, and he always feels light-hearted when he goes fishing. You see, he is just as fond of fishing as is Little Joe Otter or Billy Mink or Buster Bear. And now he was making his way through the Green Forest to the Laughing Brook, sure that by the time he had followed it down to the Smiling Pool he would have a fine lot of trout to take home. He knew every pool in the Laughing Brook where the trout love to hide, did Farmer Brown's boy, and it was just the kind of a morning when the trout should be hungry. So he whistled as he tramped along, and his whistle was good to hear.

When he reached the first little pool he baited his hook very carefully and then, taking the greatest care to keep out of sight of any trout that might be in the little pool, he began to fish. Now Farmer Brown's boy learned a long time ago that to be a successful fisherman one must have a great deal of patience, so though he didn't get a bite right away as he had expected to, he wasn't the least bit discouraged. He kept very quiet and fished and fished, patiently waiting for a foolish trout to take his hook. But he didn't get so much as a nibble. "Either the trout have lost their appetite or they have grown very wise," muttered Farmer Brown's boy, as after a long time he moved on to the next little pool.

There the same thing happened. He was very patient, very, very patient, but his patience brought no reward, not so much as the faintest kind of a nibble. Farmer Brown's boy trudged on to the next pool, and there was a puzzled frown on his freckled face. Such a thing never had happened before. He didn't know what to make of it. All the night before he had dreamed about the delicious dinner of fried trout he would have the next day, and now—well, if he didn't catch some trout pretty soon, that splendid dinner would never be anything but a dream.

"If I didn't know that nobody else comes fishing here, I should think that somebody had been here this very morning and caught all the fish or else frightened them so that they are all in hiding," said he, as he trudged on to the next little pool. "I never had such bad luck in all my life before. Hello! What's this?"

There, on the bank beside the little pool, were the heads of three trout. Farmer Brown's boy scowled down at them more puzzled than ever. "Somebody *has* been fishing here, and they have had better luck than I have," thought he. He looked up the Laughing Brook and down the Laughing Brook and this way and that way, but no one was to be seen. Then he picked up one of the little heads and looked at it sharply. "It wasn't cut off with a knife; it was bitten off!" he exclaimed. "I wonder now if Billy Mink is the scamp who has spoiled my fun."

Thereafter he kept a sharp lookout for signs of Billy Mink, but though he found two or three more trout heads, he saw no other signs and he caught no fish. This puzzled him more than ever. It didn't seem possible that such a little fellow as Billy Mink could have caught or frightened all the fish or have eaten so many. Besides, he didn't remember ever having known Billy to leave heads around that way. Billy sometimes catches more fish than he can eat, but then he usually hides them. The farther he went down the Laughing Brook, the more puzzled Farmer Brown's boy grew. It made him feel very queer. He would have felt still more queer if he had known that all the time two other fishermen who had been before him were watching him and chuckling to themselves. They were Little Joe Otter and Buster Bear.

VIII

Farmer Brown's Boy Feels His Hair Rise

'Twas just a sudden odd surprise
Made Farmer Brown's boy's hair to rise.

THAT'S A FUNNY THING for hair to do—rise up all of a sudden—isn't it? But that is just what the hair on Farmer Brown's boy's head did the day he went fishing in the Laughing Brook and had no luck at all. There are just two things that make hair rise—anger and fear. Anger sometimes makes the hair on the back and neck of Bowser the Hound and of some other little people bristle and stand up, and you know the hair on the tail of Black Pussy stands on end until her tail looks twice as big as it really is. Both anger and fear make it do that. But there is only one thing that can make the hair on the head of Farmer Brown's boy rise, and as it isn't anger, of course it must be fear.

It never had happened before. You see, there isn't much of anything that Farmer Brown's boy is really afraid of. Perhaps he wouldn't have been afraid this time if it hadn't been for the surprise of what he found. You see when he had found the heads of those trout on the bank he knew right away that some one else had been fishing, and that was why he couldn't catch any; but it didn't seem possible that little Billy Mink could have eaten all those trout, and Farmer Brown's boy didn't once think of Little Joe Otter, and so he was very, very much puzzled.

He was turning it all over in his mind and studying what it could mean, when he came to a little muddy place on the bank of the Laughing Brook, and there he saw something that made his eyes look as if they would pop right out of his head, and it was right then that he felt his hair rise. Anyway, that is what he said when he told about it afterward. What was it he saw? What do you think? Why, it was a footprint in the soft mud. Yes, Sir, that's what it was, and all it was. But it was the biggest footprint Farmer Brown's boy ever had seen, and it looked as if it had been made only

a few minutes before. It was the footprint of
Buster Bear.

Now Farmer Brown's boy didn't know that
Buster Bear had come down to the Green Forest to live. He never had heard of a Bear being
in the Green Forest. And so he was so surprised that he had hard work to believe his
own eyes, and he had a queer feeling all
over,—a little chilly feeling, although it was a
warm day. Somehow, he didn't feel like meet-
ing Buster Bear. If he had had his terrible gun
with him, it might have been different. But he
didn't, and so he suddenly made up his mind
that he didn't want to fish any more that day.
He had a funny feeling, too, that he was being
watched, although he couldn't see any one. He
was being watched. Little Joe Otter and
Buster Bear were watching him and taking
the greatest care to keep out of his sight.

All the way home through the Green Forest,
Farmer Brown's boy kept looking behind him,
and he didn't draw a long breath until he
reached the edge of the Green Forest. He
hadn't run, but he had wanted to.

"Huh!" said Buster Bear to Little Joe Otter,
"I believe he was afraid!"

And Buster Bear was just exactly right.

IX

Little Joe Otter Has
Great News to Tell

LITTLE JOE OTTER was fairly bursting with excitement. He could hardly contain himself. He felt that he had the greatest news to tell since Peter Rabbit had first found the tracks of Buster Bear in the Green Forest. He couldn't keep it to himself a minute longer than he had to. So he hurried to the Smiling Pool, where he was sure he would find Billy Mink and Jerry Muskrat and Grandfather Frog and Spotty the Turtle, and he hoped that perhaps some of the little people who live in the Green Forest might be there too. Sure enough, Peter Rabbit was there on one side of the Smiling Pool, making faces at Reddy Fox, who was on the other side, which, of course, was not at all nice of Peter. Mr. and Mrs. Redwing were there, and Blacky the Crow was sitting in the Big Hickory-tree.

Little Joe Otter swam straight to the Big Rock and climbed up to the very highest part. He looked so excited, and his eyes sparkled so, that every one knew right away that something had happened.

"Hi!" cried Billy Mink. "Look at Little Joe Otter! It must be that for once he has been smarter than Buster Bear."

Little Joe made a good-natured face at Billy Mink and shook his head. "No, Billy," said he, "you are wrong, altogether wrong. I don't believe anybody can be smarter than Buster Bear."

Reddy Fox rolled his lips back in an unpleasant grin. "Don't be too sure of that!" he snapped. "I'm not through with him yet."

"Boaster! Boaster!" cried Peter Rabbit.

Reddy glared across the Smiling Pool at Peter. "I'm not through with you either, Peter Rabbit!" he snarled. "You'll find it out one of these fine days!"

"Reddy, Reddy, smart and sly,
Couldn't catch a buzzing fly!"

taunted Peter.

"Chug-a-rum!" said Grandfather Frog in his deepest, gruffest voice. "We know all about that. What we want to know is what Little Joe Otter has got on his mind."

"It's news—great news!" cried Little Joe.

"We can tell better how great it is when we hear what it is," replied Grandfather Frog testily. "What is it?"

Reddy glared across the Smiling Pool
at Peter. *Page 30.*

Little Joe Otter looked around at all the eager faces watching him, and then in the slowest, most provoking way, he drawled: "Farmer Brown's boy is afraid of Buster Bear."

For a minute no one said a word. Then Blacky the Crow leaned down from his perch in the Big Hickory-tree and looked very hard at Little Joe as he said:

"I don't believe it. I don't believe a word of it. Farmer Brown's boy isn't afraid of any one who lives in the Green Forest or on the Green Meadows or in the Smiling Pool, and you know it. We are all afraid of him."

Little Joe glared back at Blacky. "I don't care whether you believe it or not; it's true," he retorted. Then he told how early that very morning he and Buster Bear had been fishing together in the Laughing Brook, and how Farmer Brown's boy had been fishing there too, and hadn't caught a single trout because they had all been caught or frightened before he got there. Then he told how Farmer Brown's boy had found a footprint of Buster Bear in the soft mud, and how he had stopped fishing right away and started for home, look- ing behind him with fear in his eyes all the way.

"Now tell me that he isn't afraid!" concluded Little Joe. "For once he knows just how we feel when he comes prowling around where we are. Isn't that great news? Now we'll get even with *him!*"

"I'll believe it when I see it for myself!" snapped Blacky the Crow.

X

Buster Bear Becomes a Hero

THE NEWS that Little Joe Otter told at the Smiling Pool,—how Farmer Brown's boy had run away from Buster Bear without even seeing him,—soon spread all over the Green Meadows and through the Green Forest, until every one who lives there knew about it. Of course, Peter Rabbit helped spread it. Trust Peter for that! But everybody else helped too. You see, they had all been afraid of Farmer Brown's boy for so long that they were tickled almost to pieces at the very thought of having some one in the Green Forest who could make Farmer Brown's boy feel fear as they had felt it. And so it was that Buster Bear became a hero right away to most of them.

A few doubted Little Joe's story. One of them was Blacky the Crow. Another was Reddy Fox. Blacky doubted because he knew Farmer Brown's boy so well that he couldn't imagine him afraid. Reddy doubted because he didn't want to believe. You see, he was jealous of Buster Bear, and at the same time he was afraid of him. So Reddy pretended not to believe a word of what Little Joe Otter had said, and he agreed with Blacky that only by seeing Farmer Brown's boy afraid could he ever be made to believe it. But nearly everybody else believed it, and there was great rejoicing. Most of them were afraid of Buster, very much afraid of him, because he was so big and strong. But they were still more afraid of Farmer Brown's boy, because they didn't know him or understand him, and because in the past he had tried to catch some of them in traps and had hunted some of them with his terrible gun.

So now they were very proud to think that one of their own number actually had frightened him, and they began to look on Buster Bear as a real hero. They tried in ever so many ways to show him how friendly they felt and went quite out of their way to do him favors. Whenever they met one another, all they could talk about was the smartness and the greatness of Buster Bear.

"Now I guess Farmer Brown's boy will keep away from the Green Forest, and we won't have to be all the time watching out for him," said Bobby Coon, as he washed his dinner in the Laughing Brook, for you know he is very neat and particular.

"And he won't dare set any more traps for me," gloated Billy Mink.

"Ah wish Brer Bear would go up to Farmer Brown's henhouse and scare Farmer Brown's boy so that he would keep away from there. It would be a favor to me which Ah cert'nly would appreciate," said Unc' Billy Possum when he heard the news.

"Let's all go together and tell Buster Bear how much obliged we are for what he has done," proposed Jerry Muskrat.

"That's a splendid idea!" cried Little Joe Otter. "We'll do it right away."

"Caw, caw, caw!" broke in Blacky the Crow. "I say, let's wait and see for ourselves if it is all true."

"Of course it's true!" snapped Little Joe Otter. "Don't you believe I'm telling the truth?"

"Certainly, certainly. Of course no one doubts your word," replied Blacky, with the utmost politeness. "But you say yourself that Farmer Brown's boy didn't see Buster Bear, but only his footprint. Perhaps he didn't know whose it was, and if he had he wouldn't have been afraid. Now I've got a plan by which we can see for ourselves if he really is afraid of Buster Bear."

"What is it?" asked Sammy Jay eagerly.

Blacky the Crow shook his head and winked. "That's telling," said he. "I want to think it over. If you meet me at the Big Hickory-tree at sun-up to-morrow morning, and get everybody else to come that you can, perhaps I will tell you."

XI

Blacky the Crow
Tells His Plan

Blacky is a dreamer!
Blacky is a schemer!
His voice is strong;
When things go wrong
Blacky is a screamer!

IT'S A FACT. Blacky the Crow is forever dreaming and scheming and almost always it is of mischief. He is one of the smartest and cleverest of all the little people of the Green

Meadows and the Green Forest, and all the others know it. Blacky likes excitement. He wants something going on. The more exciting it is, the better he likes it. Then he has a chance to use that harsh voice of his, and how he does use it!

So now, as he sat in the top of the Big Hickory-tree beside the Smiling Pool and looked down on all the little people gathered there, he was very happy. In the first place he felt very important, and you know Blacky dearly loves to feel important. They had all come at his invitation to listen to a plan for seeing for themselves if it were really true that Farmer Brown's boy was afraid of Buster Bear.

On the Big Rock in the Smiling Pool sat Little Joe Otter, Billy Mink, and Jerry Muskrat. On his big, green lily-pad sat Grandfather Frog. On another lily-pad sat Spotty the Turtle. On the bank on one side of the Smiling Pool were Peter Rabbit, Jumper the Hare, Danny Meadow Mouse, Johnny Chuck, Jimmy Skunk, Unc' Billy Possum, Striped Chipmunk and Old Mr. Toad. On the other side of the Smiling Pool were Reddy Fox, Digger the Badger, and Bobby Coon. In the Big Hickory-tree were Chatterer the Red Squirrel, Happy Jack the Gray Squirrel, and Sammy Jay.

Blacky waited until he was sure that no one else was coming. Then he cleared his throat very loudly and began to speak. "Friends," said he.

Everybody grinned, for Blacky has played so many sharp tricks that no one is really his friend unless it is that other mischief-maker, Sammy Jay, who, you know, is Blacky's cousin. But no one said anything, and Blacky went on.

"Little Joe Otter has told us how he saw Farmer Brown's boy hurry home when he found the footprint of Buster Bear on the edge of the Laughing Brook, and how all the way he kept looking behind him, as if he were afraid. Perhaps he was, and then again perhaps he wasn't. Perhaps he had something else on his mind. You have made a hero of Buster Bear, because you believe Little Joe's story. Now I don't say that I don't believe it, but I do say that I will be a lot more sure that Farmer Brown's boy is afraid of Buster when I see him run away myself. Now here is my plan:

"To-morrow morning, very early, Sammy Jay and I will make a great fuss near the edge of the Green Forest. Farmer Brown's boy has a lot of curiosity, and he will be sure to come over to see what it is all about. Then we will lead him to where Buster Bear is. If he runs away, I will be the first to admit that Buster Bear is as great a hero as some of you seem to think he is. It is a very simple plan, and if you will all hide where you can watch, you will be able to see for yourselves if Little Joe Otter is right. Now what do you say?"

Right away everybody began to talk at the same time. It was such a simple plan that everybody agreed to it. And it promised to be so exciting that everybody promised to be there, that is, everybody but Grandfather Frog and Spotty the Turtle, who didn't care to go so far away from the Smiling Pool. So it was agreed that Blacky should try his plan the very next morning.

XII

Farmer Brown's Boy and
Buster Bear Grow Curious

EVER SINCE it was light enough to see at all, Blacky the Crow had been sitting in the top of the tallest tree on the edge of the Green Forest nearest to Farmer Brown's house, and never for an instant had he taken his eyes from Farmer Brown's back door. What was he watching for? Why, for Farmer Brown's boy to come out on his way to milk the cows. Meanwhile, Sammy Jay was slipping silently through the Green Forest, looking for Buster Bear, so that when the time came he could let his cousin, Blacky the Crow, know just where Buster was.

By and by the back door of Farmer Brown's house opened, and out stepped Farmer Brown's boy. In each hand he carried a milk pail. Right away Blacky began to scream at the top of his lungs. "Caw, caw, caw!" shouted Blacky. "Caw, caw, caw!" And all the time he flew about among the trees near the edge of the Green Forest as if so excited that he couldn't keep still. Farmer Brown's boy looked over there as if he wondered what all that fuss was about, as indeed he did, but he didn't start to go over and see. No, Sir, he started straight for the barn.

Blacky didn't know what to make of it. You see, smart as he is and shrewd as he is, Blacky doesn't know anything about the meaning of duty, for he never has to work excepting to get enough to eat. So, when Farmer Brown's boy started for the barn instead of for the Green Forest, Blacky didn't know what to make of it. He screamed harder and louder than ever, until his voice grew so hoarse he couldn't scream any more, but Farmer Brown's boy kept right on to the barn.

"I'd like to know what you're making such a fuss about, Mr. Crow, but I've got to feed the cows and milk them first," said he.

Now all this time the other little people of the Green Forest and the Green Meadows had been hiding where they could see all that went on. When Farmer Brown's boy disappeared in the barn, Chatterer the Red Squirrel snickered right out loud. "Ha, ha, ha! This is a great plan of yours, Blacky! Ha, ha, ha!" he shouted. Blacky couldn't find a word to say. He just hung his head, which is something Blacky seldom does.

"Perhaps if we wait until he comes out again, he will come over here," said Sammy Jay, who had joined Blacky. So it was decided to wait. It seemed as if Farmer Brown's boy never would come out, but at last he did. Blacky and Sammy Jay at once began to scream and make all the fuss they could. Farmer Brown's boy took the two pails of milk into the house, then out he came and started straight for the Green Forest. He was so curious to know what it all meant that he couldn't wait another minute.

Now there was some one else with a great
deal of curiosity also. He had heard the
screaming of Blacky the Crow and Sammy
Jay, and he had listened until he couldn't
stand it another minute. He just *had* to know
what it was all about. So at the same time
Farmer Brown's boy started for the Green
Forest, this other listener started towards the
place where Blacky and Sammy were making
such a racket. He walked very softly so as not
to make a sound. It was Buster Bear.

XIII

Farmer Brown's Boy and
Buster Bear Meet

If you should meet with Buster Bear
While walking through the wood,
What would you do? Now tell me true.
I'd run the best I could.

THAT is what Farmer Brown's boy did
when he met Buster Bear, and a lot of the
little people of the Green Forest and some
from the Green Meadows saw him. When
Farmer Brown's boy came hurrying home
from the Laughing Brook without any fish one

day and told about the great footprint he had
seen in a muddy place on the bank deep in the
Green Forest, and had said he was sure that it
was the footprint of a Bear, he had been
laughed at. Farmer Brown had laughed and
laughed.

"Why," said he, "there hasn't been a Bear in
the Green Forest for years and years and
years, not since my own grandfather was a little boy, and that, you know, was a long, long,
long time ago. If you want to find Mr. Bear,
you will have to go to the Great Woods. I don't
know who made that footprint, but it certainly couldn't have been a Bear. I think you
must have imagined it."

Then he had laughed some more, all of
which goes to show how easy it is to be mistaken, and how foolish it is to laugh at things
you really don't know about. Buster Bear *had*
come to live in the Green Forest, and Farmer
Brown's boy *had* seen his footprint. But
Farmer Brown laughed so much and made fun
of him so much, that at last his boy began to
think that he must have been mistaken after
all. So when he heard Blacky the Crow and
Sammy Jay making a great fuss near the edge
of the Green Forest, he never once thought of
Buster Bear, as he started over to see what
was going on.

When Blacky and Sammy saw him coming,

they moved a little farther in to the Green Forest, still screaming in the most excited way. They felt sure that Farmer Brown's boy would follow them, and they meant to lead him to where Sammy had seen Buster Bear that morning. Then they would find out for sure if what Little Joe Otter had said was true,—that Farmer Brown's boy really was afraid of Buster Bear.

Now all around, behind trees and stumps, and under thick branches, and even in tree tops, were other little people watching with round, wide-open eyes to see what would happen. It was very exciting, the most exciting thing they could remember. You see, they had come to believe that Farmer Brown's boy wasn't afraid of anybody or anything, and as most of them were very much afraid of him, they had hard work to believe that he would really be afraid of even such a great, big, strong fellow as Buster Bear. Every one was so busy watching Farmer Brown's boy that no one saw Buster coming from the other direction.

You see, Buster walked very softly. Big as he is, he can walk without making the teeniest, weeniest sound. And that is how it happened that no one saw him or heard him until just as Farmer Brown's boy stepped out from behind one side of a thick little hemlock-tree, Buster Bear stepped out from behind the other side of that same little tree, and there they were face to face! Then everybody held their breath, even Blacky the Crow and Sammy Jay. For just a little minute it was so still there in the Green Forest that not the least little sound could be heard. What was going to happen?

XIV

A Surprising Thing Happens

BLACKY THE CROW and Sammy Jay, looking down from the top of a tall tree, held their breath. Happy Jack the Gray Squirrel and his cousin, Chatterer the Red Squirrel, looking down from another tree, held *their* breath. Unc' Billy Possum, sticking his head out from a hollow tree, held *his* breath. Bobby Coon, looking through a hole in a hollow stump in which he was hiding, held *his* breath. Reddy Fox, lying flat down behind a heap of brush, held *his* breath. Peter Rabbit, sitting bolt upright under a thick hemlock branch, with eyes and ears wide open, held *his* breath. And all the other little people who happened to be where they could see did the same thing.

You see, it was the most exciting moment ever was in the Green Forest. Farmer Brown's boy had just stepped out from behind one side of a little hemlock-tree and Buster Bear had just stepped out from behind the opposite side of the little hemlock-tree and neither had known that the other was anywhere near. For a whole minute they stood there face to face, gazing into each other's eyes, while everybody watched and waited, and it seemed as if the whole Green Forest was holding its breath.

Then something happened. Yes, Sir, something happened. Farmer Brown's boy opened his mouth and yelled! It was such a sudden yell and such a loud yell that it startled Chatterer so that he nearly fell from his place in the tree, and it made Reddy Fox jump to his feet ready to run. And that yell was a yell of fright. There was no doubt about it, for with the yell Farmer Brown's boy turned and ran for home, as no one ever had seen him run before. He ran just as Peter Rabbit runs when he has got to reach the dear Old Briar-patch before Reddy Fox can catch him, which, you know, is as fast as he can run. Once he stumbled and fell, but he scrambled to his feet in a twinkling, and away he went without once turning his head to see if Buster Bear was after him. There wasn't any doubt that he was afraid, very much afraid.

Everybody leaned forward to watch him. "What did I tell you? Didn't I say that he was afraid of Buster Bear?" cried Little Joe Otter, dancing about with excitement.

"You were right, Little Joe! I'm sorry that I doubted it. See him go! Caw, caw, caw!" shrieked Blacky the Crow.

For a minute or two everybody forgot about Buster Bear. Then there was a great crash which made everybody turn to look the other way. What do you think they saw? Why, Buster Bear was running away too, and he was running twice as fast as Farmer Brown's boy! He bumped into trees and crashed through bushes and jumped over logs, and in almost no time at all he was out of sight. Altogether it was the most surprising thing that the little people of the Green Forest ever had seen.

Sammy Jay looked at Blacky the Crow, and Blacky looked at Chatterer, and Chatterer looked at Happy Jack, and Happy Jack looked at Peter Rabbit, and Peter looked at Unc' Billy Possum, and Unc' Billy looked at Bobby Coon,

Buster Bear was running away too.
Page 47.

and Bobby looked at Johnny Chuck, and
Johnny looked at Reddy Fox, and Reddy
looked at Jimmy Skunk, and Jimmy looked at
Billy Mink, and Billy looked at Little Joe Otter,
and for a minute nobody could say a word.
Then Little Joe gave a funny little gasp.

"Why, why-e-e!" said he, "I believe Buster
Bear is afraid too!" Unc' Billy Possum chuckled. "Ah believe yo' are right again, Brer
Otter," said he. "It cert'nly does look so. If
Brer Bear isn't scared, he must have remembered something impo'tant and has gone to
attend to it in a powerful hurry."

Then everybody began to laugh.

XV

Buster Bear Is a Fallen Hero

A FALLEN HERO is some one to whom
every one has looked up as very brave
and then proves to be less brave than he was
supposed to be. That was the way with Buster
Bear. When Little Joe Otter had told how
Farmer Brown's boy had been afraid at the
mere sight of one of Buster Bear's big foot-

prints, they had at once made a hero of Buster. At least some of them had. As this was the first time, the very first time, that they had ever known any one who lives in the Green Forest to make Farmer Brown's boy run away, they looked on Buster Bear with a great deal of respect and were very proud of him.

But now they had seen Buster Bear and Farmer Brown's boy meet face to face; and while it was true that Farmer Brown's boy had run away as fast as ever he could, it was also true that Buster Bear had done the same thing. He had run even faster than Farmer Brown's boy, and had hidden in the most lonely place he could find in the very deepest part of the Green Forest. It was hard to believe, but it was true. And right away everybody lost a great deal of the respect for Buster which they had felt. It is always that way. They began to say unkind things about him. They said them among themselves, and some of them even said them to Buster when they met him, or said them so that he would hear them.

Of course Blacky the Crow and Sammy Jay, who, because they can fly, have nothing to fear from Buster, and who always delight in making other people uncomfortable, never let a chance go by to tell Buster and everybody else within hearing what they thought of him. They delighted in flying about through the Green Forest until they had found Buster Bear and then from the safety of the tree tops screaming at him.

> "Buster Bear is big and strong;
> His teeth are big; his claws are long;
> In spite of these he runs away
> And hides himself the livelong day!"

A dozen times a day Buster would hear them screaming this. He would grind his teeth and glare up at them, but that was all he could do. He couldn't get at them. He just had to stand it and do nothing. But when impudent little Chatterer the Red Squirrel shouted the same thing from a place just out of reach in a big pine-tree, Buster could stand it no longer. He gave a deep, angry growl that made little shivers run over Chatterer, and then suddenly he started up that tree after Chatterer. With a frightened little shriek Chatterer scampered to the top of the tree. He hadn't known that Buster could climb. But Buster is a splendid climber, especially when the tree is big and stout as this one was, and now he went up after Chatterer, growling angrily.

How Chatterer did wish that he had kept

his tongue still! He ran to the very top of the tree, so frightened that his teeth chattered, and when he looked down and saw Buster's great mouth coming nearer and nearer, he nearly tumbled down with terror. The worst of it was there wasn't another tree near enough for him to jump to. He was in trouble this time, was Chatterer, sure enough! And there was no one to help him.

XVI

Chatterer the Red Squirrel Jumps for His Life

IT ISN'T VERY OFTEN that Chatterer the Red Squirrel knows fear. That is one reason that he is so often impudent and saucy. But once in a while a great fear takes possession of him, as when he knows that Shadow the Weasel is looking for him. You see, he knows that Shadow can go wherever he can go. There are very few of the little people of the Green Forest and the Green Meadows who do not know fear at some time or other, but it comes to Chatterer as seldom as to any one, because he is very sure of himself and his ability to hide or run away from danger.

But now as he clung to a little branch near the top of a tall pine-tree in the Green Forest and looked down at the big sharp teeth of Buster Bear drawing nearer and nearer, and listened to the deep, angry growls that made his hair stand on end, Chatterer was too frightened to think. If only he had kept his tongue still instead of saying hateful things to Buster Bear! If only he had known that Buster could climb a tree! If only he had chosen a tree near enough to other trees for him to jump across! But he *had* said hateful things, he *had* chosen to sit in a tree which stood quite by itself, and Buster Bear *could* climb! Chatterer was in the worst kind of trouble, and there was no one to blame but himself. That is usually the case with those who get into trouble.

Nearer and nearer came Buster Bear, and deeper and angrier sounded his voice. Chatterer gave a little frightened gasp and looked this way and looked that way. What should he do? What *could* he do! The ground seemed a terrible distance below. If only he had wings like Sammy Jay! But he hadn't.

"Gr-r-r-r!" growled Buster Bear. "I'll teach you manners! I'll teach you to treat your betters with respect! I'll swallow you whole, that's what I'll do. Gr-r-r-r!"

"Oh!" cried Chatterer.

"Gr-r-r-r! I'll eat you all up to the last hair on your tail!" growled Buster, scrambling a little nearer.

"Oh! Oh!" cried Chatterer, and ran out to the very tip of the little branch to which he had been clinging. Now if Chatterer had only known it, Buster Bear couldn't reach him way up there, because the tree was too small at the top for such a big fellow as Buster. But Chatterer didn't think of that. He gave one more frightened look down at those big teeth, then he shut his eyes and jumped—jumped straight out for the far-away ground.

It was a long, long, long way down to the ground, and it certainly looked as if such a little fellow as Chatterer must be killed. But Chatterer had learned from Old Mother Nature that she had given him certain things to help him at just such times, and one of them is the power to spread himself very flat. He did it now. He spread his arms and legs out just as far as he could, and that kept him from falling as fast and as hard as he otherwise would have done, because being spread out so flat that way, the air held him up a little. And then there was his tail, that funny little tail he is so fond of jerking when he scolds. This helped him too. It helped him keep his balance and keep from turning over and over.

Down, down, down he sailed and landed on his feet. Of course, he hit the ground pretty hard, and for just a second he quite lost his breath. But it was only for a second, and then he was scurrying off as fast as a frightened Squirrel could. Buster Bear watched him and grinned.

"I didn't catch him that time," he growled, "but I guess I gave him a good fright and taught him a lesson."

XVII

Buster Bear Goes Berrying

BUSTER BEAR is a great hand to talk to himself when he thinks no one is around to overhear. It's a habit. However, it isn't a bad habit unless it is carried too far. Any habit becomes bad, if it is carried too far. Suppose you had a secret, a real secret, something that nobody else knew and that you didn't want anybody else to know. And suppose you had the habit of talking to yourself. You might, without thinking, you know, tell that secret out loud to yourself, and some one might, just might happen to overhear! Then there wouldn't be any secret. That is the way that a habit which isn't bad in itself can become bad when it is carried too far.

Now Buster Bear had lived by himself in the Great Woods so long that this habit of talking to himself had grown and grown. He did it just to keep from being lonesome. Of course, when he came down to the Green Forest to live, he brought all his habits with him. That is one thing about habits,—you always take them with you wherever you go. So Buster brought this habit of talking to himself down to the Green Forest, where he had many more neighbors than he had in the Great Woods.

"Let me see, let me see, what is there to tempt my appetite?" said Buster in his deep, grumbly-rumbly voice. "I find my appetite isn't what it ought to be. I need a change. Yes, Sir, I need a change. There is something I ought to have at this time of year, and I haven't got it. There is something that I used to have and don't have now. Ha! I know! I need some fresh fruit. That's it—fresh fruit! It must be about berry time now, and I'd forgotten all about it. My, my, my, how good some berries would taste! Now if I were back up there in the Great Woods I could have all I could eat. Um-m-m-m! Makes my mouth water just to think of it. There ought to be some up in the Old Pasture. There ought to be a lot of 'em up there. If I wasn't afraid that some one would see me, I'd go up there."

Buster sighed. Then he sighed again. The more he thought about those berries he felt sure were growing in the Old Pasture, the more he wanted some. It seemed to him that never in all his life had he wanted berries as he did now. He wandered about uneasily. He was hungry—hungry for berries and nothing else. By and by he began talking to himself again.

"If I wasn't afraid of being seen, I'd go up to the Old Pasture this very minute. Seems as if I could taste those berries." He licked his lips hungrily as he spoke. Then his face brightened. "I know what I'll do! I'll go up there at the very first peep of day to-morrow. I can eat all I want and get back to the Green Forest before there is any danger that Farmer Brown's boy or any one else I'm afraid of will see me. That's just what I'll do. My, I wish to-morrow morning would hurry up and come."

Now though Buster didn't know it, some

one had been listening, and that some one was none other than Sammy Jay. When at last Buster lay down for a nap, Sammy flew away, chuckling to himself. "I believe I'll visit the Old Pasture to-morrow morning myself," thought he. "I have an idea that something interesting may happen if Buster doesn't change his mind."

Sammy was on the lookout very early the next morning. The first Jolly Little Sunbeams had only reached the Green Meadows and had not started to creep into the Green Forest, when he saw a big, dark form steal out of the Green Forest where it joins the Old Pasture. It moved very swiftly and silently, as if in a great hurry. Sammy knew who it was: it was Buster Bear, and he was going berrying. Sammy waited a little until he could see better. Then he too started for the Old Pasture.

XVIII

Somebody Else Goes Berrying

ISN'T IT FUNNY how two people will often think of the same thing at the same time, and neither one know that the other is thinking of it? That is just what happened the day that Buster Bear first thought of going berrying. While he was walking around in the Green Forest, talking to himself about how hungry he was for some berries and how sure he was that there must be some up in the Old Pasture, some one else was thinking about berries and about the Old Pasture too.

"Will you make me a berry pie if I will get the berries to-morrow?" asked Farmer Brown's boy of his mother.

Of course Mrs. Brown promised that she would, and so that night Farmer Brown's boy went to bed very early that he might get up early in the morning, and all night long he dreamed of berries and berry pies. He was awake even before jolly, round, red Mr. Sun thought it was time to get up, and he was all ready to start for the Old Pasture when the first Jolly Little Sunbeams came dancing across the Green Meadows. He carried a big tin pail, and in the bottom of it, wrapped up in a piece of paper, was a lunch, for he meant to stay until he filled that pail, if it took all day.

Now the Old Pasture is very large. It lies at the foot of the Big Mountain, and even extends a little way up on the Big Mountain. There is room in it for many people to pick berries all day without even seeing each other, unless they roam about a great deal. You see, the bushes grow very thick there, and you cannot see very far in any direction. Jolly, round, red Mr. Sun had climbed a little way up in the sky by the time Farmer Brown's boy reached the Old Pasture, and was smiling down on all the Great World, and all the Great World seemed to be smiling back. Farmer Brown's boy started to whistle, and then he stopped.

"If I whistle," thought he, "everybody will know just where I am, and will keep out of sight, and I never can get acquainted with folks if they keep out of sight."

You see, Farmer Brown's boy was just beginning to understand something that Peter Rabbit and the other little people of the Green Meadows and the Green Forest learned almost as soon as they learned to walk,—that if you don't want to be seen, you mustn't be heard. So he didn't whistle as he felt like doing, and he tried not to make a bit of noise as he followed an old cow-path towards a place where he knew the berries grew thick and oh, so big, and all the time he kept his eyes wide open, and he kept his ears open too.

That is how he happened to hear a little cry, a very faint little cry. If he had been whistling, he wouldn't have heard it at all. He stopped to listen. He never had heard a cry just like it before. At first he couldn't make out just what it was or where it came from. But one thing he was sure of, and that was that it was a cry of fright. He stood perfectly still and listened with all his might. There it was again—"Help! Help! Help!"—and it was very faint and sounded terribly frightened. He waited a minute or two, but heard nothing more. Then he put down his pail and began a hurried look here, there, and everywhere. He was sure that it had come from somewhere on the ground, so he peered behind bushes and peeped behind logs and stones, and then just as he had about given up hope of finding where it came from, he went around a little turn in the old cow-path, and there right in front of him was little Mr. Gartersnake, and what do you think he was doing? Well, I don't like to tell you, but he was trying to swallow one of the children of Stickytoes the Tree Toad. Of course Farmer Brown's boy didn't let him. He made little Mr. Gartersnake set Master Stickytoes free and held Mr. Gartersnake until Master Stickytoes was safely out of reach.

XIX

Buster Bear Has a Fine Time

BUSTER BEAR was having the finest time he had had since he came down from the Great Woods to live in the Green Forest. To be sure, he wasn't in the Green Forest now, but he wasn't far from it. He was in the Old Pasture, one edge of which touches one edge of the Green Forest. And where do you think he was, in the Old Pasture? Why, right in the middle of the biggest patch of the biggest blueberries he ever had seen in all his life! Now if there is any one thing that Buster Bear had rather have above another, it is all the berries he can eat, unless it be honey. Nothing can quite equal honey in Buster's mind. But next to honey give him berries. He isn't particular what kind of berries. Raspberries, black-berries, or blueberries, either kind, will make him perfectly happy.

"Um-m-m, my, my, but these are good!" he mumbled in his deep grumbly-rumbly voice, as he sat on his haunches stripping off the berries greedily. His little eyes twinkled with enjoyment, and he didn't mind at all if now and then he got leaves and some green berries in his mouth with the big ripe berries. He didn't try to get them out. Oh, my, no! He just chomped them all up together and patted his stomach from sheer delight. Now Buster had reached the Old Pasture just as jolly, round, red Mr. Sun had crept out of bed, and he had fully made up his mind that he would be back in the Green Forest before Mr. Sun had climbed very far up in the blue, blue sky. You see, big as he is and strong as he is, Buster Bear is very shy and bashful, and he has no desire to meet Farmer Brown, or Farmer Brown's boy, or any other of those two-legged creatures called men. It seems funny, but he actually is afraid of them. And he had a feel-ing that he was a great deal more likely to meet one of them in the Old Pasture than deep in the Green Forest.

So when he started to look for berries, he made up his mind that he would eat what he

could in a great hurry and get back to the
Green Forest before Farmer Brown's boy was
more than out of bed. But when he found
those berries he was so hungry that he forgot
his fears and everything else. They tasted so
good that he just had to eat and eat and eat.
Now you know that Buster is a very big fellow, and it takes a lot to fill him up. He kept
eating and eating and eating, and the more he
ate the more he wanted. You know how it is.
So he wandered from one patch of berries to
another in the Old Pasture, and never once
thought of the time. Somehow, time is the
hardest thing in the world to remember, when
you are having a good time.

Jolly, round, red Mr. Sun climbed higher and
higher in the blue, blue sky. He looked down
on all the Great World and saw all that was
going on. He saw Buster Bear in the Old Pasture, and smiled as he saw what a perfectly
glorious time Buster was having. And he saw
something else in the Old Pasture that made
his smile still broader. He saw Farmer
Brown's boy filling a great tin pail with blueberries, and he knew that Farmer Brown's
boy didn't know that Buster Bear was anywhere about, and he knew that Buster Bear
didn't know that Farmer Brown's boy was
anywhere about, and somehow he felt very

sure that he would see something funny happen if they should chance to meet.

"Um-m-m, um-m-m," mumbled Buster Bear with his mouth full, as he moved along to another patch of berries. And then he gave a little gasp of surprise and delight. Right in front of him was a shiny thing just full of the finest, biggest, bluest berries! There were no leaves or green ones there. Buster blinked his greedy little eyes rapidly and looked again. No, he wasn't dreaming. They were real berries, and all he had got to do was to help himself. Buster looked sharply at the shiny thing that held the berries. It seemed perfectly harmless. He reached out a big paw and pushed it gently. It tipped over and spilled out a lot of the berries. Yes, it was perfectly harmless. Buster gave a little sigh of pure happiness. He would eat those berries to the last one, and then he would go home to the Green Forest.

XX

Buster Bear Carries Off the Pail
of Farmer Brown's Boy

THE QUESTION IS, did Buster Bear steal Farmer Brown's boy's pail? To steal is to take something which belongs to some one else. There is no doubt that he stole the berries that were in the pail when he found it, for he deliberately ate them. He knew well enough that some one must have picked them—for whoever heard of blueberries growing in tin pails? So there is no doubt that when Buster took them, he stole them. But with the pail it was different. He took the pail, but he didn't mean to take it. In fact, he didn't want that pail at all.

You see it was this way: When Buster found that big tin pail brimming full of delicious berries in the shade of that big bush in the Old Pasture, he didn't stop to think whether or not he had a right to them. Buster is so fond of berries that from the very second that his greedy little eyes saw that pailful, he forgot everything but the feast that was waiting for him right under his very nose. He didn't think anything about the right or wrong of helping himself. There before him were more berries than he had ever seen together at one time in all his life, and all he had to do was to eat and eat and eat. And that is just what he did do. Of course he upset the pail, but he didn't mind a little thing like that. When he had gobbled up all the berries that rolled out, he thrust his nose into the pail to get all that were left in it. Just then he heard a little noise, as if some one were coming. He threw up his head to listen, and somehow, he never did know just how, the handle of the pail slipped back over his ears and caught there.

This was bad enough, but to make matters worse, just at that very minute he heard a shrill, angry voice shout, "Hi, there! Get out of there!" He didn't need to be told whose voice that was. It was the voice of Farmer Brown's boy. Right then and there Buster Bear nearly had a fit. There was that awful pail fast over his head so that he couldn't see a thing. Of course, that meant that he couldn't run away, which was the thing of all things he most wanted to do, for big as he is and strong as he is, Buster is very shy and bashful when human beings are around. He growled and whined and squealed. He tried to back out of the pail and couldn't. He tried to shake it off and

couldn't. He tried to pull it off, but somehow
he couldn't get hold of it. Then there was
another yell. If Buster hadn't been so frightened himself, he might have recognized that
second yell as one of fright, for that is what it
was. You see Farmer Brown's boy had just
discovered Buster Bear. When he had yelled
the first time, he had supposed that it was one
of the young cattle who live in the Old Pasture
all summer, but when he saw Buster, he was
just as badly frightened as Buster himself. In
fact, he was too surprised and frightened even
to run. After that second yell he just stood
still and stared.

Buster clawed at that awful thing on his
head more frantically than ever. Suddenly it
slipped off, so that he could see. He gave one
frightened look at Farmer Brown's boy, and
then with a mighty "Woof!" he started for the
Green Forest as fast as his legs could take
him, and this was very fast indeed, let me tell
you. He didn't stop to pick out a path, but just
crashed through the bushes as if they were
nothing at all, just nothing at all. But the fun-
niest thing of all is this—he took that pail
with him! Yes, Sir, Buster Bear ran away with
the big tin pail of Farmer's Brown's boy! You
see when it slipped off his head, the handle
was still around his neck, and there he was

running away with a pail hanging from his neck! He didn't want it. He would have given anything to get rid of it. But he took it because he couldn't help it. And that brings us back to the question, did Buster steal Farmer Brown's boy's pail? What do you think?

XXI

Sammy Jay Makes Things Worse for Buster Bear

"THIEF, THIEF, THIEF! Thief, thief, thief!" Sammy Jay was screaming at the top of his lungs, as he followed Buster Bear across the Old Pasture towards the Green Forest. Never had he screamed so loud, and never had his voice sounded so excited. The little people of the Green Forest, the Green Meadows, and the Smiling Pool are so used to hearing Sammy cry thief that usually they think very little about it. But every blessed one who heard Sammy this morning stopped whatever he was doing and pricked up his ears to listen.

Sammy's cousin, Blacky the Crow, just happened to be flying along the edge of the Old

Pasture, and the minute he heard Sammy's voice, he turned and flew over to see what it was all about. Just as soon as he caught sight of Buster Bear running for the Green Forest as hard as ever he could, he understood what had excited Sammy so. He was so surprised that he almost forgot to keep his wings moving. Buster Bear had what looked to Blacky very much like a tin pail hanging from his neck! No wonder Sammy was excited. Blacky beat his wings fiercely and started after Sammy.

And so they reached the edge of the Green Forest, Buster Bear running as hard as ever he could, Sammy Jay flying just behind him and screaming, "Thief, thief, thief!" at the top of his lungs, and behind him Blacky the Crow, trying to catch up and yelling as loud as he could, "Caw, caw, caw! Come on, everybody! Come on! Come on!"

Poor Buster! It was bad enough to be frightened almost to death as he had been up in the Old Pasture when the pail had caught over his head just as Farmer Brown's boy had yelled at him. Then to have the handle of the pail slip down around his neck so that he couldn't get rid of the pail but had to take it with him as he ran, was making a bad matter worse. Now to have all his neighbors of the Green Forest see him in such a fix and make fun of him, was more than he could stand. He felt humiliated. That is just another way of saying shamed. Yes, Sir, Buster felt that he was shamed in the eyes of his neighbors, and he wanted nothing so much as to get away by himself, where no one could see him, and try to get rid of that dreadful pail. But Buster is so big that it is not easy for him to find a hiding place. So when he reached the Green Forest, he kept right on to the deepest, darkest, most lonesome part and crept under the thickest hemlock-tree he could find.

But it was of no use. The sharp eyes of Sammy Jay and Blacky the Crow saw him. They actually flew into the very tree under which he was hiding, and how they did scream! Pretty soon Ol' Mistah Buzzard came dropping down out of the blue, blue sky and took a seat on a convenient dead tree, where he could see all that went on. Ol' Mistah Buzzard began to grin as soon as he saw that tin pail on Buster's neck. Then came others,— Redtail the Hawk, Scrapper the Kingbird, Redwing the Blackbird, Drummer the Woodpecker, Welcome Robin, Tommy Tit the Chickadee, Jenny Wren, Redeye the Vireo, and ever so many more. They came from the Old Orchard, the Green Meadows, and even down by the Smiling Pool, for the voices of Sammy Jay and Blacky the Crow carried far, and at the sound of them everybody hurried over, sure that something exciting was going on.

Presently Buster heard light footsteps, and peeping out, he saw Billy Mink and Peter Rabbit and Jumper the Hare and Prickly Porky and Reddy Fox and Jimmy Skunk. Even timid little Whitefoot the Wood Mouse was where he could peer out and see without being seen. Of course, Chatterer the Red Squirrel and Happy Jack the Gray Squirrel were there. There they all sat in a great circle around him, each where he felt safe, but where he could see, and every one of them laughing and making fun of Buster.

"Thief, thief, thief!" screamed Sammy until his throat was sore. The worst of it was Buster knew that everybody knew that it was true. That awful pail was proof of it.

"I wish I never had thought of berries," growled Buster to himself.

XXII

Buster Bear Has a
Fit of Temper

A temper is a bad, bad thing
When once it gets away.
There's nothing quite at all like it
To spoil a pleasant day.

BUSTER BEAR was in a terrible temper.
Yes, Sir, Buster Bear was having the
worst fit of temper ever seen in the Green
Forest. And the worst part of it all was that all
his neighbors of the Green Forest and a whole
lot from the Green Meadows and the Smiling
Pool were also there to see it. It is bad enough
to give way to temper when you are all alone,
and there is no one to watch you, but when
you let temper get the best of you right where
others see you, oh, dear, dear, it certainly is a
sorry sight.

Now ordinarily Buster is one of the most
good-natured persons in the world. It takes a
great deal to rouse his temper. He isn't one
tenth so quick tempered as Chatterer the Red
Squirrel, or Sammy Jay, or Reddy Fox. But
when his temper is aroused and gets away

from him, then watch out! It seemed to Buster that he had had all that he could stand that day and a little more. First had come the fright back there in the Old Pasture. Then the pail had slipped down behind his ears and held fast, so he had run all the way to the Green Forest with it hanging about his neck. This was bad enough, for he knew just how funny he must look, and besides, it was very uncomfortable. But to have Sammy Jay call everybody within hearing to come and see him was more than he could stand. It seemed to Buster as if everybody who lives in the Green Forest, on the Green Meadows, or around the Smiling Brook, was sitting around his hiding place, laughing and making fun of him. It was more than any self-respecting Bear could stand.

With a roar of anger Buster Bear charged out of his hiding place. He rushed this way and that way! He roared with all his might! He was very terrible to see. Those who could fly, flew. Those who could climb, climbed. And those who were swift of foot, ran. A few who could neither fly nor climb nor run fast, hid and lay shaking and trembling for fear that Buster would find them. In less time than it takes to tell about it, Buster was alone. At least, he couldn't see any one.

Then he vented his temper on the tin pail.

Those who could fly, flew. Those who
could climb, climbed. *Page 74*.

He cuffed at it and pulled at it, all the time growling angrily. He lay down and clawed at it with his hind feet. At last the handle broke, and he was free! He shook himself. Then he jumped on the helpless pail. With a blow of a big paw he sent it clattering against a tree. He tried to bite it. Then he once more fell to knocking it this way and that way, until it was pounded flat, and no one would ever have guessed that it had once been a pail.

Then, and not till then, did Buster recover his usual good nature. Little by little, as he thought it all over, a look of shame crept into his face. "I—I guess it wasn't the fault of that thing. I ought to have known enough to keep my head out of it," he said slowly and thoughtfully.

"You got no more than you deserve for stealing Farmer Brown's boy's berries," said Sammy Jay, who had come back and was looking on from the top of a tree. "You ought to know by this time that no good comes of stealing."

Buster Bear looked up and grinned, and there was a twinkle in his eyes. "You ought to know, Sammy Jay," said he. "I hope you'll always remember it."

"Thief, thief, thief!" screamed Sammy, and flew away.

XXIII

Farmer Brown's Boy
Lunches on Berries

When things go wrong in spite of you
To smile's the best thing you can do—
To smile and say, "I'm mighty glad
They are no worse; they're not so bad!"

THAT IS WHAT Farmer Brown's boy said when he found that Buster Bear had stolen the berries he had worked so hard to pick and then had run off with the pail. You see, Farmer Brown's boy is learning to be something of a philosopher, one of those people who accept bad things cheerfully and right away see how they are better than they might have been. When he had first heard some one in the bushes where he had hidden his pail of berries, he had been very sure that it was one of the cows or young cattle who live in the Old Pasture during the summer. He had been afraid that they might stupidly kick over the pail and spill the berries, and he had hurried to drive whoever it was away. It hadn't entered his head that it could be anybody who would eat those berries.

When he had yelled and Buster Bear had suddenly appeared, struggling to get off the pail which had caught over his head, Farmer Brown's boy had been too frightened to even move. Then he had seen Buster tear away through the brush even more frightened than he was, and right away his courage had begun to come back.

"If he is so afraid of me, I guess I needn't be afraid of him," said he. "I've lost my berries, but it is worth it to find out that he is afraid of me. There are plenty more on the bushes, and all I've got to do is to pick them. It might be worse."

He walked over to the place where the pail had been, and then he remembered that when Buster ran away he had carried the pail with him, hanging about his neck. He whistled. It was a comical little whistle of chagrin as he realized that he had nothing in which to put more berries, even if he picked them. "It's worse than I thought," cried he. "That bear has cheated me out of that berry pie my mother promised me." Then he began to laugh, as he thought of how funny Buster Bear had looked with the pail about his neck, and then because, you know, he is learning to be a philosopher, he once more repeated, "It might have been worse. Yes, indeed, it might have been worse. That bear might have tried to eat me instead of the berries. I guess I'll go eat that lunch I left back by the spring, and then I'll go home. I can pick berries some other day."

Chuckling happily over Buster Bear's great fright, Farmer Brown's boy tramped back to the spring where he had left two thick sandwiches on a flat stone when he started to save his pail of berries. "My, but those sandwiches will taste good," thought he. "I'm glad they are big and thick. I never was hungrier in my life. Hello!" This he exclaimed right out loud, for he had just come in sight of the flat stone where the sandwiches should have been, and they were not there. No, Sir, there wasn't so much as a crumb left of those two thick sandwiches. You see, Old Man Coyote had found them and gobbled them up while Farmer Brown's boy was away.

But Farmer Brown's boy didn't know anything about Old Man Coyote. He rubbed his eyes and stared everywhere, even up in the trees, as if he thought those sandwiches might be hanging up there. They had disappeared as completely as if they never had been, and Old Man Coyote had taken care to leave no trace of his visit. Farmer Brown's boy gaped foolishly this way and that way. Then, instead of growing angry, a slow smile stole over his freckled face. "I guess some one else was hungry too," he muttered. "Wonder who it was? Guess this Old Pasture is no place for me to-day. I'll fill up on berries and then I'll go home."

So Farmer Brown's boy made his lunch on blueberries and then rather sheepishly he started for home to tell of all the strange things that had happened to him in the Old Pasture. Two or three times, as he trudged along, he stopped to scratch his head thoughtfully. "I guess," said he at last, "that I'm not so smart as I thought I was, and I've got a lot to learn yet."

This is the end of the adventures of Buster Bear in this book because—guess why. Because Old Mr. Toad insists that I must write a book about his adventures, and Old Mr. Toad is such a good friend of all of us that I am going to do it.*

THE END.

*NOTE: *The Adventures of Old Mr. Toad* is not published by Dover Publications.

CHILDREN'S THRIFT CLASSICS

Just $1.00
All books complete and unabridged, except where noted.
96pp., 5³/₁₆″ × 8¼″, paperbound.